AF584333

Bonny grows her feathers and learns to fly

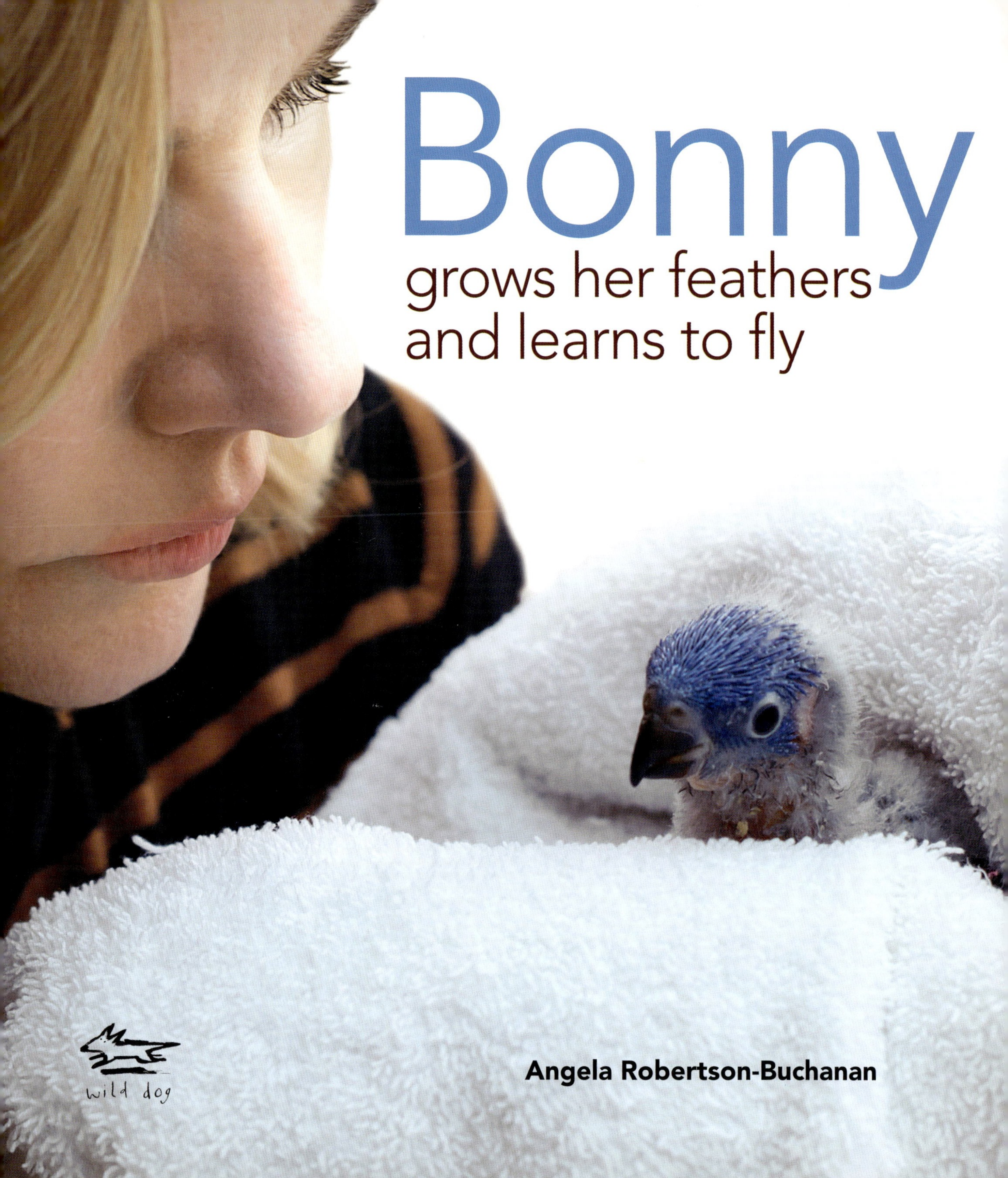

Angela Robertson-Buchanan

wild dog

Bonny's mother laid her egg in a tree hollow. Rainbow lorikeet eggs take about 24 days to hatch. Not long after Bonny hatched she fell out of the tree.

Day 1

A passer-by found Bonny and brought her to me. She was covered in fine wispy hair.

Day 2

Rainbow lorikeets are born with their eyes closed. Bonny's eyes were still completely closed two days after hatching.

Adult lorikeets eat nectar from flowers and feed it to their young. Baby lorikeets raised by humans need to be fed a special mix of homemade nectar. This was fed to Bonny every two-and-a-half hours during the day.

Day 4

Bonny was unable to hold her head up on her own, as her muscles were not strong enough.

Day 12

Bonny started opening her eyes. It took several days before she could open them properly.

Day 23

Bonny's eyes were now completely open, and she could hold her head up by herself.

Day 36

Bonny had grown thick, fluffy down feathers on her body. On her head were blue pin feathers, which would eventually develop into adult feathers.

Pin feathers are covered in a protective sheath of keratin. This sheath is long and narrow like a pin. Keratin is the same stuff our fingernails are made of.

Day 51

Bonny's colourful wing feathers had now started to grow.

Day 60

When Bonny's feathers were almost fully grown, the keratin sheath protecting them began to peel away. This let her feathers begin to fluff out.

Day 65

Bonny had grown almost all of her feathers.

Day 70

Bonny started to test out her wings.

Day 80

Bonny became more inquisitive as she grew older. She was nearly ready to be released into the wild.

Rainbow lorikeets are born with a black beak. As they mature, their beak gradually becomes less black. When they are a fully grown adult their beak is bright orange and red.

Day 90

When Bonny could fly strongly and was able to find the right foods to eat in the wild, I released her.

Bonny joined up with a flock of lorikeets that lived nearby.

Lorikeets are flock birds, which means they hang out in groups of birds of the same type. During the day they move around with 20 to 30 other lorikeets. At sunset they join up with even more lorikeets – sometimes as many as 1000 birds.

Bonny still visits me from time to time.

First published in 2015 by
wild dog
54A Alexandra Parade
Clifton Hill Vic 3068
Australia
+61 3 9419 9406
dog@wdog.com.au
wdog.com.au

Angela was born in England and graduated from Portsmouth University with a degree in Art, Design and Media. She went on to work in photography-based jobs for over 15 years before moving to Australia, where she fell in love with the native flowers, plants and animals, but especially in love with the birds. She trained as a wildlife rescuer and carer for Sydney WIRES, and specialises in the care and rehabilitation of birds. This has given her a unique opportunity to gain the birds trust and create intimate portraits, revealing perspectives that are rarely explored. Angela has won awards and held many exhibitions. She and her husband Scott share their home with a cockatoo named "Casper" and two crazy galahs, all of which were rescue birds.

Printed and bound in China by Everbest Printing Co. Ltd

National Library of Australia
Cataloguing-in-Publication data:
Author: Robertson-Buchanan, Angela.
Title: Bonny grows her feathers and learns to fly / Angela Robertson-Buchanan.
ISBN: 9781742033693 (hbk)
Target Audience: For primary school age.
Subjects: Rainbow lorikeet--Juvenile literature.
Rainbow lorikeet--Australia.
Dewey Number: 636.6865

10 9 8 7 6 5 4 3 2 1 15 16 17 18 19

Wild Dog would like to thank Neil Conning for his careful fact checking and thorough proofreading.